Tamara Dumas was born and raised in a small town in Estonia. Soon after completing her university studies, she moved to London in pursuit of a career in life coaching.

While You Were Awake is her first book. She is currently working on her second, "TH!NK", which will be the first instalment in a planned series.

While You Were Awake

TAMARA DUMAS

While You Were Awake

Vanguard Press

VANGUARD PAPERBACK

© Copyright 2015
Tamara Dumas

The right of Tamara Dumas to be identified as author of
this work has been asserted by her in accordance with the
Copyright, Designs and Patents Act 1988.

A CIP catalogue record for this title is
available from the British Library.

ISBN 978 178465 0117

All characters in this book are fictitious, and any resemblance
to actual persons living or dead is purely coincidental.

Vanguard Press is an imprint of
Pegasus Elliot Mackenzie Publishers Ltd.
www.pegasuspublishers.com

First Published in 2015

Vanguard Press
Sheraton House Castle Park
Cambridge England

Printed & Bound in Great Britain

Acknowledgements

I would like to thank my dear friends who have offered me a great support in writing the book and, more important, shared their experiences with me. My special acknowledgement to Mindy Goff, who spent many hours proofreading my notes and writings and whose comments and suggestions I found very valuable. Special thanks to Ilsiyar and Marco, long talks with whom inspired me to look on the story from different viewpoints and search for true reason behind every event.

Last, but not the least, I would like to thank all those who inspire and encourage me to continue with the story and it is thanks to them that I look forward to the future.

PART ONE

I

21.13

All begins right here, in a restaurant with hazy light. Today I wear Hermes jour Eau De Merveilles Parfum, an iconic perfume by an extraordinarily symbolic brand. The scent of the ancient messenger-god, the god of logos, hidden wisdom and self-pleasure who has been known to this world by many names and has always been an object of worship under one name or another. Today I wear Hermes and with him I feel like an incarnated diva to say the least.

I struggle to remember the name of my companion today but it really doesn't matter, not for me anyway. We met a few times and exchanged texts, but he is saved in my phone under the name of the place we met so I don't call him by name; he is just another ticket for a fun evening and I anticipate it will be spectacular. As I unfold the plain white starched napkin to cover my knees I am trying to think what is so special about this place for the Mr Sketch. Why did he decide to invite me here? I also think I would be lucky to remember the name of this place in a couple of weeks' time. All the restaurants seem far too alike for me lately with their matching cutlery and napkins set on the tables; they are so absurdly similar from venue to venue that it has become hard to distinguish any particular place from the dozens. In other words, just a usual evening; everything has long become one bright blurred splash of something boring.

Meanwhile the waiter girl brings a curvy pitcher of still water to the table and the condensation from the surface of the cooled glass instantly leaves a round mark on the table cover. As she bends slightly over the table to pour me a glass and lights a candle the disturbingly familiar fragrance tickles my nose. Uncontrollably an alarming anxiety slowly starts crawling up my veins. The sweet scent of patchouli and white musk accompanied by light notes of pink pepper, iris and jasmine briskly carries me away to memories of one particular evening.

I am seventeen again, out with my school mate, Sofia who wore the very same perfume as this young lady today. I suppose I called her my best friend back then. It doesn't necessarily mean she was, rather it was useful for us to stick together – my appearance attracted men's attention and she knew how to benefit from it. That's what made us a good team, or at least, I believed us to be back then.

Someone pulls my hand and I become dismayed by the way the evening has developed. I catch the eye of my friend from across the room and dramatically convey to her that what started as a usual evening has become increasingly out of control and I am not happy about it. She smiled as if patronising me and said it will all be fine; I am much too naïve for my age.

The way Sofia sees it we must stay close to our new friends at all cost. They are obviously 'mad about us' and will do anything to keep us excited. She tells me that we have a reservation at a private club tonight and the chauffeur will pick us up at eleven p.m. It goes without saying that I won't have to worry about my ID or my age; doors have a way of opening for us, always.

'You really should be more easy-going if you want to get anywhere in this life,' she says, 'and you'd better get there quick while you are still young and pretty. It won't do harm if Marc looks after you, would it? Besides, it looks like he is really serious about you,' she winks teasingly. 'Seriously, get this silly crap off your mind and learn how to use your assets!'

Seeing my hesitation she adds, 'After all, one night spent together is not necessarily a reason for a relationship; you can always say that you don't remember anything from the night and then just hit up on his more handsome buddy!' She laughs with enthusiasm.

I would have trusted Sofia with my life back then, and oh my, I certainly trusted her when it came to relationships and partying. This average looking girl had everything I could ever dream of: trendy outfits, a Mini Cooper for her eighteenth birthday, which by the way was a gift from one of her many wealthy admirers, invites to the hottest parties and even the envy of all her mates. And you know what, anyone would choose to follow her and of course, I did.

She moves closer at the same time as this rampant guy who gropes me at the waist, declaring me his possession for the night. Sofia's perfume shoots up my nose and I almost start to choke.

'Just drink some more and I will take care of the rest,' she whispers. She offers me her half-filled glass with some unknown brown coloured spirit and ushers me to get on with it.

I downed the whole drink in one go, just to brush off the hostile sensation of disgust. I hated her that very moment so badly, and I hated our swaggering friends just as much as I hated the whole idea of having to succumb to someone for very doubtful pleasure.

I used to replay that evening in my mind over and over again with all different variations of my reaction. I always managed to triumph in my imagination, then I simply stopped bothering and the memory of that evening gradually disintegrated for, what I was hoping would be forever.

We were best mates for three wild years until one day I simply forgot to call her; she also forgot. I suppose our friendship just exhausted itself. It was odd, there were no arguments or drama between us – we just parted. I phoned her couple of months later but neither of us suggested to meet. We continued to speak every now and then and I was excited to tell her about my virtues: who had I met, the new clubs I had visited and all the broken relationships I added to my somewhat sophisticated collection.

At the age of twenty-three she died in a terrible car accident, despite her belief that she would live forever (she even used to use the Egyptian symbol of eternal life – Ankh ☥ – in place of the 'f' in her name). They say it was drunk driving and I am not surprised; she lived her life literally as if there were no tomorrow. But one thing is for sure, she will definitely be forever young. Hmm, damn destiny has a wicked sense of humour.

The first thing I felt was devastation as if I was torn apart. I realised then that for my whole life I had played her double and now that the prima donna was dead, I had no role of my own. I still blame myself for never finding the strength to choose my own path; to stand my ground and tell her how it actually felt like. A revelation from somewhere above, with perfect understanding, crushes in on me; it is now clear as day that ever since then the whole world had taken advantage of me, exploiting my weakness – the inability to stand my ground. Even today I continue to do what is expected of me rather than what I want; in fact, I'm not sure what it is I want anymore.

The waitress unexpectedly breaks my reverie and I am thrust back to reality.

'What would you like for a drink, madam?'

Damn, more than anything else I want to see Sofia and profess all I think about her and about that night. It was a pivotal moment in my life and I can only wish to have made different choices. I want to scream out loud that this was all against my will and how bit by bit I gave in to her superficial games and how breaking away from this vicious circle seems just impossible; it's almost like I am so hopelessly dependant on my starring role. I can't imagine living my life any differently even if it makes me sad to the point where I can literally feel physical pain. But it will never change; I will need to live with memory of this for the rest of my life. Sofia will never apologise or make it back. She left me broken, slashing my perception of the world and walked away from it all without a sense of responsibility. Gracious me, how cynical I must sound, but this is exactly how I feel right now!

The sensation of total helplessness strangles me so tightly that it gets harder to breathe. I pick up the glass of water and take several big sips, quenching the parched desert in my mouth; I place the glass down on the table, my hand shaking and spilling it all over the place.

I surely look awful now and I can see the embarrassment on the face of my companion. I can clearly read in his eyes something to the effect: 'Oh gosh, why can't you just behave normally? I pay the bloody bill and you dare to make me look foolish in public.' I can only think of one legitimate excuse to hide my shame:

'My apologies – I have asthma. Do you mind if I pop out to take my medication and get some fresh air? Please don't be upset, everything is awesome, I will be back shortly.'

He noticeably didn't believe my plea; I must be far too transparent. He says he will order some wine to start with and I suggested Calvados before running down the stairs to get out of that place.

II

21.27

The sky is pitch-black to the east while western skies still bear some remnants of twilight. The street is lit with display windows of haute couture and a few banners of various colours and size. The night is alive with the occasional passers-by; all of whom seem to be in groups out for a fun night. They are laughing and chatting with gusto and I can't help but feel they are actually mocking me. As if they have the right to judge me! Stupid people. It feels like they look at me with sarcasm and turn away quickly as soon as I gawk back. I must resist a great urge to stop each and every one of those strangers and tell them my personal vision of that evening. The story that has been buried under a thick layer of dust for so long and now, unearthed and threatening to screw my evening.

I decide that I need one shot of something strong to get me back in shape. I know he will be waiting for me back upstairs. Although the guy is not young, nor is he attractive, but he bought me a pair of Christian Loubutin shoes the other week and I don't feel right about leaving him like that. C'mon Hermes, disclose to me his name for goodness' sake!

Next door seems to be a decent pub and so I decide that it would be the best place for a quick rehab of my feelings, unless of course Sofia wants to make her way back to this world to face the truth?

21.31

I arrive inside the overcrowded pub and the heat tints my face red; I wish I hadn't grabbed my jacket on the way out of restaurant.

I move straight to the bar and, seeing all these people queuing, I take out a crisp twenty pound note and slide it over to the bartender.

'One Sambuca, please.' I pause. 'Make that a double. Keep the change.' Works like a charm every time.

It's noisy in here; all the blue collars around me are mingling and having a good time. They are obviously talking shop, but I can't make a single word out of their raucous chatter.

Despite the place being nicely furnished it is still a pub, with a strong odour of beer that freezes all my senses. Someone steps on my shoe while from other side I feel kick in my side with an elbow.

'Sorry, luv.'

If he would only know how much these shoes are worth he would probably be more considerate but you just can't expect it from everybody, not in this place anyway. In situations like that

I always face a dilemma – my only thought is to clean that dirt off my beloved shoe and say something rude in return; yet every time I have to pretend I am not bothered at all.

'Hey, it's only shoes, leave it.' I take it as a triumph over myself, almost like a manifestation of my carelessness of anything material; or at least that's what other people think.

I take a moment to examine the people around me. I don't normally go to these sorts of places and everything seems so different to what I am used to; a whole new planet right around the corner!

My mind is desperately seeking something to catch onto; to live out my bitter frustration and to my satisfaction there is plenty. Next to me is a group of mates; empty glasses scattered all over the place and you can see they're already pretty pissed. With my Sambuca in hand, I lean over and blend into their group. I swear, if someone would walk in to the pub that very second they would have decided I came with these chaps.

In my opinion there can't be a more demeaning thing than being in the company of men who choose to wear those cheap grey suits from high street stores. No offence, but they're baggy and shapeless and have no texture, they do nothing to flatter; loose on the buttocks and boring formless folds. Okay wait; there can be something worse – the faded ornate socks with bobbles that this chap is flashing under his trousers. Yep, not all outfits are created equal!

One guy is louder than all the rest; he had a bit too much. He waves his hands and describes how embarrassing it was last week to lie drunk on the floor in the middle of the living room while the kids were watching TV; definitely not my cup of tea. I think of this poor man in his late forties, shopping for a new outfit with his lovely wife, asking for her opinion. The suit sits awfully and the colour reminiscent of a miserable London sky in autumn.

She nods,

'Looks great on you! Take it…'

Eek, I can justify just about anything, but I can't rationalize bad taste.

I fire a smile across to the bartender and make my way to grab another shot. I down it quickly and the sweet Sambuca burns my lips; I close my eyes and breathe in slowly. 'All is marvellous, I am fine,' I repeat three times in my mind like a mantra. By that time I was already distracted from the palpable sense of self-worthlessness. Three, four, five more counts and a pleasant warmth fills my entire body, I feel much better now.

On my way out, resisting the urge to laugh, I compliment the guy on his socks.

He smiles. 'Do you really? I got them from Next.'

I giggle compulsively. 'Whatever.'

21.45

I am happy to be back in restaurant.

'Sorry for making you wait, Alistair.' Of course it's Alistair, how could I forget? He ordered nice flowers for me the other week and the courier mentioned Alistair. 'I feel much better now. Are we ready to order?' I take a sip of calvados and smile warmly, I am happy that I don't have to spend my evening in the pub downstairs with a pint of cider. And it doesn't matter if he is almost twice my age. I am glad my life has gone the way it has and I have eliminated any possibility of getting into a long nerve-racking relationship with some miserable guy who would rather believe in ill stars than take control of his own life. Will this bliss last for long?

Thinking of how to make him feel special I bend over the table to adjust his colourful expensive looking necktie, not the best idea with deep cleavage, but I realise it a bit too late for that now when I catch his glance full of lust. Oh, well…

Best way to find out if a man has taste is to see what kind of necktie he is wearing and how it is tied – given that it was him who tied it of course!

I personally believe though that it is pure women's business to tie the cravat. This has been passed down for centuries and women were the ones who knew the elusive tie magic. I am fascinated by the idea that ties have always represented some mysterious forces, and in some ways, even formed the destiny. I can professionally tie eleven knots so I suppose that I am well prepared for tying the knot with my one and only; just need to find him.

His necktie is set in a fully symmetric Windsor – not the hardest from my collection, still, not a task for graduates. The fabric is textured and colours are bright just the way I like. White, purple and dark green stripe diagonally across; my hand slips down the grainy fabric. I sense his cologne full of cedar wood and tobacco notes with hints of bergamot and frankincense – very masculine and convincing. Alcohol is working its magic with my mind very softly and I'm my usual self again, in control of the situation.

III

The venue is one of those fancy restaurants where you will never get full because of the laughable portion sizes. However, if you are after sophisticated gourmet and want to amuse your sense of taste with the combination of various savours in a multitude of forms and proportions then this place is for you. I have to give Alistair that credit, he has a good taste when it comes to food… and ties.

I myself can eat almost anything due to the fact that I can't stand cooking at home. My regular dish is leafy salad "washed and ready to eat" more often than not skipping on the dressing. I can go as far as to make oven cooked salmon and espresso, but that's about it. And why would you need anything else if you can have delicious meals full of heavenly goodness at your avail within minutes?

Since during the week I mainly eat plain food without much excess, I really enjoy my wines-and-dines in restaurants. Tonight our meals are bursting with flavour and look deliciously mouth-watering. The menu could probably make a high contender in my personal top twenty if only the dishes would be a bit bigger.

I eat *primi* and *secondi* without saying much; I am trying to focus my entire attention on the assembly of tastes and aromas skilfully combined by the chef, like an artisan mixes paints for his masterpiece. I am particularly pleased by the texture and taste of the foie gras. It is hard to find a decent one in restaurants as most of them serve it as a very soft pâté, whereas I am big fan of solid textured foie gras that is fried without losing its original texture. Prepared in this way it better complements the beef and adds more dimensions to the flavour.

It's funny, every time I eat goose liver I think of Prometheus whose liver will forever be pecked by the eagle. Is it somewhat a payback of fowl to humankind? Would the mythical eagle stop eating Prometheus' liver and end his torture if all humans would stop tormenting birds and killing them for theirs? I doubt that I will ever get to see that day, so the mystery remains still; perfect righteousness yet to be perceived by my conscious mind.

My rapture is somehow overthrown by absolutely irrelevant questions and stories. Alistair is being nosy and wants to know what's new in my life and by the sound of it he is only interested in one particular thing. I answer only with short sentences and it is clear to me that he is not quite happy with my responses. He would be much more content to hear a monologue capturing every detail of how I spent time with my ex last week, and what is my opinion on the book that he suggested I must read.

Honestly, he is dauntingly boring person; one who is searching for someone to entertain him for his money. In his imagination I am a sort of contemporary and a more cosseted version of old world French courtesans who must be well educated and knowledgeable, speak a few languages fluently and be comfortable talking on any subject the master deems. I would have thought I had seen enough to be able to recognise this type of attitude within seconds, yet I hope that I am wrong this time and he might genuinely be interested. It is rather remarkable how I always believe what I want to, as opposed to what common sense and the statistical data of my past experiences proves things to be.

I am trying not to rush with my food, but yet I finish it way too quickly, even before the pre-heated plate has cooled. I know I should leave some food on my plate, it's just common courtesy, but today I am just so hungry; besides, the food is so great I can't resist.

Next comes the dessert with double macchiato – a bit too late for coffee, but I don't plan to sleep any time soon. The caramelised-white-chocolate ice cream with a slice of fried bacon is served on a rectangular white plate and is decorated with sprinkles of tiny fresh lavender flowers. It is almost impossible to imagine how well these two complement each other. The ice cream releases new notes of flavour as it melts in the mouth. The strong smoky caramel blows on the tongue prevailing over any sweet taste of white chocolate. When the caramel flavour eases, there is a final adagio of salty fried bacon; real indulgence for those who hunt new gastro experiences. I close my eyes and inhale the smell of fresh and fruity wine to complete the experience.

22.54

By the time we are done I have added one calvados, about two glasses of white wine and a shot of Limoncello.

'Are you feeling better now?' Alistair asks. 'I have prepared a special surprise for you tonight, but only if you feel like it.' He takes my hand and kisses it very softly.

IV

I live alone in a flat owned by one of my wealthy friends; I suppose I can call him a friend as it didn't go much further than that. Although he has several flats in top spots around the world he is not particularly good at looking after them. As far as I know they all stand empty, full of memories from previous owners… spooky.

Once I paid him a visit in his London flat while he was sorting some business with locals. I liked the apartment and he liked me so we agreed I would stay and look after the flat while he was away. I hoped it had meant a relationship; I was wrong.

Apparently, he was just looking for a live-in housekeeper as he doesn't bother to come to London frequently. Not even my much appealing lingerie has persuaded him to visit this place more often. Shame nothing good has come out of it, I really like the charisma and modesty about him – something that I am clearly lacking.

I promised him I would behave and look after his flat, and that I do well. No friends or even the occasional house party; the place is dead silent and empty most of the time. I get in touch with him every month; he is a very likeable guy indeed, always worrying about his Italian style garden and pays the landscaper to trim the decorative bushes and grass.

The garden is the only thing I really love about this flat. It's the only place I share with other inhabitants – birds and squirrels. The rest is always silent and motionless like on those black and white pictures of strangers playing volleyball on the beach – one of the customary illustrations in the numerous frames that I never managed to change for photos of my dear ones. I love to come to the garden whenever the weather is nice and watch how the wind plays with petals, carrying seasonal smells around. I have already learned to guess where the wind comes from by the scent it brings. I have an entire area mapped in my mind; what a useless skill indeed.

I can't stand solitude for long and that's why I never hurry home. After a while of being on my own I feel like I am going mad; all the nasty thoughts and painful memories line up to nudge me. Self-blame and self-pity served boiling hot are just about the only dishes I can prepare from scratch in minutes and evenings like that are the worst. If I manage to get home conscious I will always find a reason to break into tears while no one can see, fuelling my sobering loneliness with big greedy mouthfuls… There is no doubt in my mind; whatever this evening brings me, it's best to hang out for a couple more drinks.

'Yes, sure, I feel splendid, what did you plan for me? Knowing you it must be something spectacular, I can't wait to see!' I soundlessly clap my hands in excitement. I am getting actually thrilled about the surprise and can't wait to rush into a cab that will whisk us somewhere remarkable. I feel great and ready to swing in tune with summery house well into the morning and even further than that. I will be happy to update my contact list with a couple more Mr Novikovs or Mr Tramps and everything tonight will be amazing.

The evening has only just begun for me.

V

23.10

As soon as we get in to the cab he opens his wallet and pulls out a folded fifty pound note.

'Here, take it in case you will need a cab home later.' I pull it slowly out of his hand and put the note inside my bra.

'Got it, catch a cab.' I touch his cheek gently with my cheek, imitating a kiss, and a bunch of hair, lavishly sprayed with perfume, slips down my shoulder closer to his face. He inhales slowly, moving my hair out of his way and plants a kiss on my skin. Not the most pleasant feeling of all; I brush revulsion away with laughter.

'Oh you're such a gentleman, Alistair. Tell me more about the place we are going to, I want to know everything.' I slip down the seat a bit and stretch my legs in the cab giving a rest to my feet; those red-soled stilettos are damn hard to walk in!

'Be patient and don't worry, you're going to hate it.' He laughs and kisses my hand. 'Just joking, this is the most elite place in London you probably haven't even heard of.'

For the rest of the journey I sit quietly trying to think whether he was really joking and why it was meant to be funny. And what the hell is this "elite" club that "I have never heard of?'

23.27

We stop outside an ostentatious mansion somewhere in the heart of Soho. There is no queue to get in and it looks like one of the finest private clubs. I ask Alistair what is the name of this place; he whispers in my ear something about kittens.

As we venture inside we are asked to leave our jackets in the cloakroom and to put the masks on that were provided. I choose the see-through lace bunny mask that covers half of my face while Alistair picks a red devil that only covers his eyes. Although I can still see everything through my bunny mask it gives me a whole different feeling, as if I am different person now, an enigmatic seductive stranger.

We enter the main room and I see a bohemian looking supply of mostly younger guys and girls, the trail of wealth and filth emanating from their half-naked bodies. We came quite late as I understand, as all sorts of things are happening around me. Some sip champagne, some make love with one or several partners; men are mainly wearing smart suits, while women don corsets or enticing cocktail dresses.

Music is playing very softly as the main background hums are clinking glasses and quiet conversation. The prevalent scent of spicy wood fills the entire room and it feels very discreet here; something just implies on atmosphere of open mindedness yet total secrecy. I am enthralled by the decadence, an almost Bacchanalian ambiance. I have never before seen anything like this; a club with hushed music and folks having intercourse in every corner. Frankly I am a bit puzzled by the whole thing. Strangely, it doesn't cause discomfort, thanks to the atmosphere of some mutual trust that prevails here, I feel like I am in the company of old friends where no one will judge you. I want to get introduced to all of them, moreover; I feel I could make some good long-standing friends here.

I take a chance and ask Alistair once again,

'What is this club called?'

He says it's "Killing Kittens". To my reaction to the name he says it's very funny because it refers to common saying that every time a woman pleasures herself God kills a kitten. I nod with a smile. I have heard this joke before and thinking of those tiny cute creatures being killed because a limited number of men are capable of satisfying their woman, I don't find it funny at all! Nevertheless, I am not surprised, the name is chosen in the best traditions of Soho.

I suggest we should move and check out upstairs but he cuts me off.

'It is not time yet. We will stay downstairs for a while, if you don't mind. I am waiting for some friends.'

At that moment I am not in mood to argue, I am happy to mingle for a while and get to know these folks better. I am getting excited from what can come out of our new friendship – I can almost see coming wild parties on luxury yachts, shopping in the south coast of France.

'Sure, let's wait for your friends!'

We join the other people downstairs with our glasses of champagne, from the open bar – something any club *must* have in my opinion.

A few people come over to acknowledge us and kindly introduce themselves, with nicknames, I suppose. Too many weird names for one place! I have almost certainly recognised one prominent artist whose work I used to follow a couple of years ago. I am not surprised to meet him in this setting; the internet is full of his naked selfies and some more hardcore ones from right in the shooting studio. Intrigued by the rank of attendees I feel the virtue; being among moguls in this laid-back setting is what I love most.

As I am wearing the mask I feel very comfortable and the fizzy champagne is working well. I drink in the atmosphere for a while, enjoying the music and small chit-chat with my new friends. They seem to be extremely courteous and it feels really good. I would say their behaviour is a bit more tantalising than I would expect to see in a club but, I suppose, it is explained by the setting. I also try this role on; I seek for physical contact with people around and the sensation of their skin under my fingers is electrifying. Strong fragrances are amusing my mind and acting as some sort of hypnotic scents as we all move in response to each others' body language like the flute snakes move in response to their master's movements. I find myself totally absorbed by the setting and by the phenomenon of connectedness with all others.

Looking at all those around me, I think that everything is way too surreal, we are all in the right places and there doesn't seem to be any negativity like you would see in other clubs. It feels like I am a part of some movie – a rather captivating one with perfectly matched film crew who make everybody believe it is for real. The only thing that worries me is that all those spread a bit further away are eyeing me up as if choosing the target for the night. And although they try to hide their intentions, it still stands out and I find it overwhelming. I am trying to hide my distress from the fact that I am considered to be merely a prize for the night, first of all from myself.

In effort to escape the dissecting looks of others I put my hand on Alistair's shoulder; I wrongly thought it would help. Instead he takes it as permission and in response he puts his masculine hand on my hip without being distracted from conversation.

He smooches me just like a kitten and his excessive attention is getting irritating to say the least. My mood changes radically within mere seconds. I start to have this funny feeling that he invited me over here and wants to show off to his mogul friends what are fined doll he's got for the night, before taking me to his bedroom, and it just doesn't sit well with me. I know for sure that I am only going home from here and nowhere else, yet all around will definitely assume we are a couple. I feel as though my dignity is being compromised and what's worse, for nothing in return.

I can't think of anything better other than insisting we should go upstairs, I want to see the entire place before sneaking away.

'Please, let me check upstairs, I am really keen.' Seeing a hint of hesitation in his eyes I add, 'I will be a good girl, promise.' This phrase always works, whatever it might mean for men, and it just worked yet again.

01.33

We leisurely move upstairs where the bar is decorated with ornate mirrors and chandeliers, to the back there is a massive jacuzzi where I see one busty nude young lady with a big colourful tattoo on her lower back having fun with three handsome men; an almost unbelievable view. I really have to pinch myself and make extra effort to keep my jaw from dropping!

A bit further down I also see a huge bed that is occupied by at least a dozen naked bodies interwoven to the point where nothing makes sense anymore. It looks more like a snakes' nest with everybody moving in slow motion; they are obviously having a good time and are not even bothered by those watching from the side lines in anticipation.

Even further down there are some private rooms for those who value discretion. There is one with door wide open and I can see three girls having à ménage a trois on the couch; no men in that private suite as far as I can see.

For a moment I think I have had too much alcohol or, perhaps, it is Alistair who added something in my glass. I have heard it happen with some vulnerable, inexperienced party girls. But how on earth could it happen to me? I carefully skim off only the most elegant men with a sense of dignity and at least some modesty. How could Alistair do that to me? No, he surely didn't. I brush my doubts away; it is happening for real, it is really happening!

I am rather shaken by the sight of so many people wearing nothing but face masks. Heavens, help me out of here! Now more than ever before everything seems so surreal. Something I never would have imagined seeing right in the heart of London; something so incredibly hedonistic and blatant. The idea of such *creepy* fun simply never even crossed my mind before! Sure, I am not an innocent girl and never claimed to be, but this place took me beyond all thinkable borders that my upbringing has engrained within my psyche.

I feel like I am not even myself anymore, not the one that crossed the threshold of this building. I all of a sudden realise that I am not the same girl that finished college with distinctions and went for a first job interview with a city law firm. I am not the same girl who cared about her friends and family; I can't even think when the last time I spoke to my parents was or to my college mates; I have crossed them out of my life. Thinking about it, I am not the same girl who won each and every marathon at school, overcoming my weaknesses and setting new standards. Looks like the only standards I can set now are far below what I would go for back then. Nothing is left from me, from my past aspirations or morals and the worst part is that I don't even know myself anymore. The new me simply took over and forgot to introduce herself. I can only learn to know myself all over again and, hopefully, I will like what there is to discover.

I keep moving forward with my hand on Alistair's shoulder. Grunts of pleasure are reaching me from every corner and some singles are just watching from the sides in their comfortable armchairs. A few are enjoying the company of young attractive ladies on their laps, sliding back and forth in slow motions. Men are noticeably having strong erections but, as explained by Alistair, they are not allowed to approach unless invited to.

We reach the rear corner of the room from where everything happening around can be overseen. We join the table busy with few couples and young girls who are having a chat, sitting on comfortable red suede armchairs. One bottle of champagne and a bottle of vodka are resting in a big cooler filled with ice; three juice pitchers surrounding the cooler. We exchange names and I ask Alistair to mix me a strong vodka cocktail; only strong spirit can get me through that hell.

Two girls sharing the same armchair are kissing passionately and are not paying any attention to us. Generally, all of Alistair's friends look very confident and appear to be long-standing members who couldn't be surprised by absolutely anything. From the multitude of Venetian masks I'm getting a flashback from the Venice carnival with the only difference that these people here are wearing significantly less clothes.

Now I am absolutely convinced that these sorts of parties are most definitely taking place at the secret venues during the Venice carnival, too; common tourists have simply never been told about it in travel guides. Moreover, I suspect that sexual pretext was the main aim in defining the Venetian tradition, just the same as Bacchanalia – there is nothing new under the sun.

We all wear masks and no one will ever recognise us tonight. While tomorrow we can go to work and, perhaps, meet the same people with whom we had intercourse last night, somewhere on a business meeting; no one will ever say a word, no one will ever know.

I am distracted from my thoughts by one perfectly pampered girl; I think she said her name is Gemma. She clearly considers me to be the potential partner for the night and so she tests the ground by asking in a no-pressure manner what kind of things I am into. By this time my good swinging mood I had downstairs is vanished and I literally force myself to be polite. I am trying to be nice to the young lady but it is getting harder to hide my anxiety and disgust. I have heard of these sort of places before but to visit one was never on my To Do list.

Now, when I have seen most of the venue I can leave the place with a sense of accomplishment. I will meet tomorrow with my friends and can casually mention the Killing Kittens, almost as if I am a long standing member. It will surely make them speak about me – but first I need to make it home. At a most appropriate point, in my view, I cut the girl off and excuse myself to the toilet.

On my way to ladies' room I spot one transvestite standing right next to the curtained window, touching herself. She is wearing only tiny black underwear with rosy decorations and a black feathered mask that covers her eyes. All about her is somehow edgy; you can clearly see it is a guy despite her full natural-looking silicone boobs; silicone just like mine, fake like everything else in my life. She turns her head towards me and our eyes meet for a second while she puts a finger in her mouth and starts sucking it slowly. Gee, all I want is to close my eyes and open them in some better place. Not daring to look around, I follow the lines on the timber floor up until I reach the door of the ladies' room.

I hope to finally get a breather and think of the best way to sneak out. The washroom is lit by the dim light of metre high pillar candles in the corner with condoms laid all around for those who might decide to give it a go. Red interior with small

Chesterfield couches at the sides; two couples lacking any semblance of clothes are having sex without any awareness.

Embarrassed by the view I try to look away and get laughed at by one young attractive participant; a girl with thick, long hair. She stands up and comes closer while her hair falls down her shoulders like a waterfall, covering her upper torso. Her body demonstrates everything we should be going to the gym for – slender, fit physique with washboard abs and toned thighs. The girl slowly grabs my hand and places it on her waist leaving me wanting to shrink and disappear. From her demeanour I can't get whether she wants to make me feel good or she is just mocking me for being so cowardly in their presence.

I smile politely trying to hide my anger, take my hand off her and rub it against my bum as if cleaning dirt from it.

'Sorry, I think I had too much today.' I escape to the cubicle.

02.36

So here I am, hiding in the ladies' room surrounded by some perverts who could surely be diagnosed with some psychical disorders. I sit on the lid of the toilet pot and finally take a minute to clean my shoes. Exactly as I thought – a few new scratches are shining right at the front of the polished black shoe and by the look of it this pair is going to be recycled tomorrow. There will be nothing left to me by tomorrow from hanging out with

Alistair, even this pair of shoes won't last much longer; what a waste of time.

'What are you doing here, girl?' I whisper to myself. I understand that it might be cool to attend this sort of place, kind of showing that you belong. But according to what's happening inside my mind now, this is not the place I want to belong to. My heart is racing from the mix of alcohol with coffee and from an overwhelming feeling of helplessness. Why do I always find myself being a victim of the situation? I must stop it and I must act now while it is not too late. I make myself a new resolution—to not to be a dupe ever again; fix my make up looking into the reflecting advert on the door in front of me and walk out of the cubicle with snobby grace making sure that no white paper has stuck to my shoes. Still remembering the tacky skin of hers I wash my hands twice with soap; no naked bodies can make me shy anymore – I am not even paying attention to what is going on in the corner on the couch, none of my business.

I get out of the rest room and move back to the table, paying demeaning looks to girls around me and absolutely ignoring men. I get closer to the cosy table in the rear corner where a few moments ago were Alistair's friends. By this point some have left the table already, leaving only my companion and another pretty-looking well-groomed young lady in her early thirties wearing burlesque lingerie under a black club blazer. I see them kissing friskily and I think for a moment I am saved for the night, I can safely sneak out from this bedlam.

Oddly, I don't feel in any way upset about the fact that Alistair has mingled; moreover, I feel extremely happy. Happy because I wouldn't need to do something I don't want; happy because I can leave this place and just go home without explanations or feelings of guilt. I will delete Alistair's number straight after closing the door of this horrible place behind my back and will go home and, taking into account the amount of consumed alcohol, I have good odds of forgetting everything that is happening here together with Alistair. I smile… truly, happily, from the bottom of my heart.

When I have come close enough I take Alistair's hand and am about to say I am leaving while he embraces me and pulls closer to his hip. As he does that I feel strong erection inside his trousers; I am actually quite surprised he still has them on unlike the majority of the visitors. The girl in the burlesque underwear comes closer to my back and places her soft hands on my shoulders, inviting me to take part in their affair. For some reason it feels like they have staged it and I am somehow trapped between two bodies longing for sex.

It is as clear as day that it was Alistair's only goal for the evening – to get me drunk and bring me here where I would get titillated from simply looking around and would beg him to take advantage of me right here, in this pandemonium. It is evident he planned to bend me over right here, no need to go anywhere else; how convenient – less hassle, maximum outcome. As additional bonus to his virtue he would demonstrate to his plutocrats-mates how hot he still is. And it goes without saying that my personality doesn't mean anything for him, he doesn't consider me to be a real life human being with feelings and thoughts.

'I can't believe how perverted you actually are, Alistair!'

I pull him away aggressively and shout to him to get off me; the girl behind me was apparently ready for my reaction as she moved out of my way in a split second. She now stands by Alistair's side as if she is somehow not related to what is going on between me and him.

'Are you okay?' Alistair asks with embarrassment. 'Your childish behaviour is embarrassing to say the least.' His tone changes to patronising, probably in the hope that it will have calming impact on me.

I suppose it's a very British thing to say you are just fine regardless of whatever your state of mind is. Britons have always been the subject of humorous remarks concerning their way too civilised mind-set. I wonder what makes us say 'I am okay' in the moments of a painful agony, delirium of the spirit. Why do we make choices that are not serving us well? It is quite obvious that by saying 'I'm fine' we avoid dealing with the problem or, rather, deny the existence of the problem itself. We pull on the porcelain masks of hard-headed I-couldn't-care-less kind of folks who can never get hurt and are in total control of the situation.

Sadly, it lasts only until we get home or meet our friends — here comes the whimper and all the bitterness gets exposed because our little ugly ambitions start talking aloud, crying and fighting for existence in our minds; they finally grow into suffocating monsters, too big to deal with...Just for couple of hours. We swallow our own poisonous saliva by the end of the monologue and we're back to square one, ready to put up with almost anything. Who suffers? I suppose our friends suffer more than anyone else or, in my case, tonight it might be my mirror.

'Nothing is okay,' I say quietly, surprised that I actually said that. I understand that this is the point of no return. Now, when I have opened my mouth I have to tell everything. 'Nothing is okay, don't you understand?' I look in his face, covered with the diabolic mask, it perfectly fits the purpose – my mind takes him rather as symbol, the representation of all indecent men I have had to deal with. 'Meeting a girl who is half your age for a quickie in a club is not okay, do you follow? Inviting a lady to a dodgy, perverted sex club just so that you don't have to take Viagra tonight is also not okay.'

I try to put my storming thoughts and feelings into plain words and it is not as easy as I thought it would be. I go on:

'It is not okay that you expect me to be in a good mood every time we chat or meet. Nor is it okay that I have to act the way you wish or speak only on your preferred subjects at a time convenient, again, only for you! I am a human being for goodness' sake and I reserve the right for the expression of my bloody feelings, whether you like it or not. And you will never buy this right off me. Not for all your money.

'The fact that I am treated merely like a fancy accessory for your night is not fine and will never be.' It feels like I can't stop anymore and it doesn't matter if I exaggerate something; he would have gotten there sooner or later.

Although I speak very loudly, almost shout, no one seems to be bothered by that; everybody is busy with their affairs. In a moment of personal drama it is weird to see how everything around is just flowing as usual, no one is even paying attention. People are mostly drunk and relaxed; they talk and smile, kissing or having intercourse right in a club on a massive, decadent bed.

My breath speeds up and I am now almost hysterical while I go on.

'I am sick of your texts that I am expected to respond to and pretend I am at all interested. The only reason I do all that is out of sense of pity for you, a lonely miserable debauch. Are you getting it? You are not a macho with pots of money as you probably used to be. You are not young, nor are you attractive anymore! You must face it, there can only be two reasons why a lady half your age would keep in contact with you – money and pity; and I don't know which one is worse in your case.' I take a breath and think what else to add.

'I am genuinely sorry for you that you still believe your fantasy of being attractive, successful and butch. And I am sorry that you suffer from maddening loneliness, (may be a bit too maddening at your age, eh?) but I have no intention of fostering your illusions further, seriously. Come down to earth and start treating people with respect they deserve for goodness sake!

'I will tell you more – I know you hate me now for telling you the truth because I must be the only one person in your rich worthless life who got the courage to open their mouth. Now you hate me and I just don't care anymore, you are not anybody I would take seriously, listen or care about. I am only a piece of meat for you and you don't deserve any better handling than you get!'

During my tirade he never said a single word, even his facial expression, as much as I could see under the mask, didn't change. He looks like he hears it every day or simply dismisses my opinion just because I have had a few drinks. Alistair looks straight into my eyes with his cold look, like a serpent before attack. Gosh, I must look awful now, what can be worse than woman arguing with a guy? Only a smashed woman arguing with a guy in sex club.

I see everything in slow motion and silent right now. I see the girl in the blazer and underwear staring at me in total stupor and another couple on the right side of the table whispering to each other, something exciting and then breaking into silent laughter a second later. I can clearly see everything that is happening on the huge bed in the centre of the room; also in slow motion – every emotion and every pronounced word caught in my mind. I feel the pause is getting somewhat awkward.

The hot tears start falling down my face, tears of pity for myself rather than for him. This poor bloke with a wrecked life most likely made the same mistake as I – chose success to personal happiness. I can only agree it is much easier to hit the goal if you have one. It is incredibly easy to achieve anything within our system; just need to know the rules and work hard. It is, however, much harder to build up a lasting relationship.

There is no general rules that will work, no books or magazines will ever give you the right recipe. Your friends are even worse because they will only tell what *you* want to hear. More often than not you will have to sacrifice your freedom and lifestyle and it may turn back on you; at least that what happens to me all the time. You try so very hard and by doing so it appears that you are just making things worse, up until the moment that one says, 'I am leaving you.'

From my personal experience I know how painful it can be in one relationship and being always cautious of consequences I prefer to stay away as long as I can even though the loneliness is not doing me any good either. I know that Alistair is just the same.

'I hate to say but I can't be with you any longer... It is not about you; you don't deserve such cheek as me, you deserve someone better.' He goes.

It is my ex-boyfriend who ran off with the girl next door. He cheated on me while I was looking after my parents during a hard period in their lives and now tries to convince me that I deserve someone better. Turning facts inside out he makes it appear as if he actually cares about me. Bullshit, I know that all he cares about is to get rid of me with few consequences for him.

Ever since we met I have sacrificed all I had, my friends, my network. I even changed my job just because he thought my handsome colleague is hitting on me. I stopped going to my favourite shows and exhibitions and became too boring for him, too domesticated. I stopped wearing tempting clothes so that he doesn't have his jealous paranoia attacks and after a while he said that we don't have that chemistry between us. I went to the gym to keep in shape and he claimed I don't spend time with him; the list can go on.

Everything was painfully wrong in our relationship but it became the norm and it sucked me in – I couldn't think of letting him go then. I was trying even harder and every time my effort drove us further apart. And now he sits here admitting that he cheated on me searching for easy way out.

I was furious then and Shift + Deleted him from my life; it took me a long time to get over and to start enjoying my life again.

Know that, been there.

I quickly wipe warm tears off my cheeks below the mask with one hand and trying to not to look at Alistair I pour vodka in my glass and drink it at once.

'Now, excuse me, I have better things to do.' I grab my bag and leave the place pushing some people out of my way. At the door I turn back briefly expecting to see him upset – the same brunette, now wearing nothing but black and purple high waist burlesque knickers, is on her knees in front of him; his hand on her head... Sickening.

I run quickly down the stairs, some people turn around just to make sure their privacy is not under threat. While I move towards the exit his friend from downstairs sees me leaving in tears. He comes closer, his shirt is open and loose, the gilded mask is covering half of the face, and his lips are full and red from the lipstick. He asks what has happened and if there is anything that he could do. I tell him, in response to which he puts a crispy business card in the pocket of my jacket.

'Call me tomorrow, I am sure we can fix that.'

'Do you even know what you mean?'

He never said a word, just watched me, baffled, as I am walking out.

VI

Once on the street I am trying to grab as much fresh air as I can. I refuse the taxi that the doorman offers me; it is really best to have a short walk. My tight stilettos are not meant for a long walk so I just turn round the corner and sit on the bench covered with some occasional drops of water from the night drizzle. I don't care if my coat gets wet or if I will get cold, I just don't care; it is nice to sit still and observe the world from the height of new awareness, albeit so bitter.

Here, outside, there is a whole different atmosphere; a few modest couples of young boys are hanging around holding each other's hands and kissing coyly; how naïve and romantic they seem to me now. They are blissfully oblivious to what is going on just around the corner from here and I can say by the tenderness in their eyes that they really believe in love, it's not all just about sex.

One of young guys was charmed by my ridiculous bunny mask that I still have on.

'Hey, this is really nice mask, where did you get it? Are you a playboy bunny or something?' I tell him he can have it.

'Just don't go round that corner there with that mask, my girlfriends might think it's me and try to, you know, try to kiss you and stuff.' I wind him up hoping to save his world from that place. I so wish he won't be disappointed in relationships and will keep believing in love for lifetime and all that.

It started bucketing again and I hide inside the mini cab.

04.40

I get out of the taxi, anxious about the evening. Too many thoughts are pulsating in my mind, too much information for one night. I look around – it would have been beautiful early morning if I was a bit more sober. I look up in the skies and see light fluffy clouds covering the heaven like Belgium handmade lace. When was the last time I looked into the skies trying to search out amusing familiar patterns? Feels like too many years ago.

While gold sunlight is crawling slowly down the facades I decide to sit on the marble stairs outside my house on a quiet cul-de-sac street; it's better than going in anyway. Everything is asleep like in fairyland and I feel I can almost stop the moment and simply sit here and enjoy the golden daybreak forever. The dawn is the most innocent time of the day; it gives me the hope that not everything is as bad as it appears at night.

I take off my killer shoes and hold them in right hand while I rest my tired swollen feet in a small puddle left from the night's drizzle to refresh and give them a rest. I think how fun it was being a little kid, to watch the skies and splash the puddles all around.

I still remember from my school assignment that swines can't look up and never get to see the sky. At the moment I read it in an encyclopaedia this fact shook me – I was a dreamer back then, always looking up to the skies and couldn't imagine how one must spend all life looking to the ground. Now I must have become a sort of swine myself who is not capable of looking up, who won't have aspirations of any kind just because it doesn't know better; I will rather spend my time sitting in the warm puddle. I never thought about it that way before and it makes me laugh.

I smear the rainwater up my legs.

'That's it, looks more like truth,' I say to myself. Really, what is there humane and sincere within me? There surely is a lot, I just can't concentrate right now; all I can do is laugh.

I start to chuckle and gradually it grows into open laughter. I think of that madhouse down in Soho and about those people who cover their faces with masks out of fear of being revealed. I think of those young boys with my bunny mask who probably read too much of *yaoi* manga. I can't stop laughing and even don't want to try.

I laugh at Alistair, who might end up this night with some contagious add-ons and on that silly joke about the kittens. I sincerely laugh at myself. All this hair do and dramatic make up that took me an hour, sexy clothes; all that just to be hiding in a toilet cubicle. Just think of that! I am so full of nonsense, hard to even imagine, leave alone stop laughing.

My shoulders are shaking from laughter and I start feeling nauseous; I must run to the toilet.

VII

Once I am inside the flat I again experience this daunting attack of loneliness. I strip off all my clothes and turn on the shower trying to wash off all the filth I must have soaked in today. A long-forgotten fifty pound note falls down to the bath tub. For a moment I can't understand where it come from but then a flashback from a cab – Alistair gave it to me "in case I need a cab back home". It wasn't just for a cab after all, was it?

It makes me think of what soap I'd better use to wash off those labels that others hung on me in a club tonight as well as all the other labels that people have been tagging on me all my life. These are not the labels on the tubes of lotions that you just pour water over and they are gone; here I need something revolutionary new.

I suppose I've been trying to get rid of those gluey tags and labels for a good few years now. Although you can wash just about anything off with my favourite ambrosia soap, nothing seems to be working for the soul or, at least, for the memory. Sometimes I think that memory is my greatest advantage and also my greatest curse. I can't help but keep remembering something I would rather forget – it always sits here, right in my head and whispers, whispers, whispers. I have the special place for all the most formidable memories and they don't even have to be triggered; they are always an open wound.

I start speaking aloud as if there is someone listening for me inside the bathroom.

'Please let me forget this day'… and the burden of labels wrongly placed on me won't hurt me tomorrow. 'If only I can forget one night I will be definitely one step happier, maybe even happier than I was yesterday morning. Maybe tomorrow I will be able to break my habit to act as I am expected to and then, then I will start all over again, most likely.'

I rub my eyes in attempt to wash off the mascara and salty tears that are running down my cheeks again. I feel absolutely shattered; all my body is aching. I slide down the shower booth, embrace both knees with my hands and start crying like a kid, allowing running water to wash off my thoughts and memories along with the pain.

VIII

DREAM

When I was a little girl I used to enjoy the state of between being awake and falling into a deep sleep. This state lasted usually for only a couple of moments and I was trying to prolong it as much as I possibly could. I would float in my thoughts that, I knew for sure, I would fail to recall a second later and was drawing various pictures in my imagination. The atmosphere around me felt like one big down pillow that I could safely sink into. The moment when my child's mind couldn't resist the sleepiness any longer I always used to experience a scary sensation of being dragged somewhere. It was captivating for me and daunting at the same time. I was somehow very afraid of that experience and was scared to discover where it would take me. After a short while, being petrified on the unknown, I would wake up suddenly from what was becoming an overwhelming struggle and then fall asleep straightaway skipping this spine-chilling state.

At some point, when I decided I am already grown up enough (at about five), I have allowed myself to go with this force in my dreams and what I discovered amazed me. I was seeing dreams that appeared to be so real; I was having conversations with adults on serious subjects and was sharing my daily experiences with considerate entities. I couldn't find an explanation to that then, nor do I have it now. On the contrary, in the real world I had to deal with silly childish talks of other kids and grownups who were talking to me as if they were my age.

The difference was tremendous and it was hard for a child to cope with such a drift. I wasn't sure what is normal anymore, was it me or was it everybody else instead? It puzzled me; concern was always blinking at the back of my mind fading at times and then reappearing again every time I tried to share my experience with others, with no success. In the end I came to the conclusion that there is something terribly wrong with this world. I was curious why in real life people couldn't be wise and understanding. Why in real life the kids can't be intelligent and thoughtful. Why do I have to communicate with the little no-brainers my mates, and if I don't I will get 'rewarded' with concerned look of my mum who was getting preoccupied and upset about me. The worst part was that in all my explanations it is rather 'them' who are not normal which made her even more apprehensive. I was also wondering how come that such dreams were so alien for my friends or the people I looked upon – everybody just seemed to be so pigeonholed and not ready to listen to me or accept my personality for who I was, so I finally gave up trying to explain anything and took the situation for granted. I found only one outlet to my frustration as I became a sarcastic and arrogant teenager who got disillusioned with life before even getting to taste it.

I suppose this cynical nature has helped me to survive all along and saved me lots of tears and sleepless nights. Up until now I still have a special relationship with my dream and except for times when I overdo it with alcohol I see very vivid visions.

This time I discovered myself in a long queue surrounded by people of all ages, races and social backgrounds– they are queuing with me. The queue goes as far as I can see and a loud murmur comes from every side. All around me folks are having arguments and active discussions; older people explaining something to those who looks at least a bit younger. They look somewhat cheesy in their attempts to enlighten youngsters because they are standing in the very same queue so, I suppose, they don't know better – it looks like they just care about staying in the line while eliminating the competition.

In front of me I see one elegant young lady with Mediterranean features; I would say her build up is very attractive. She has a long neck that bears some ten odd golden chains and charms which she deliberately exposes for public view as much as she can. However, once I look in her eyes I soon realise that she is a perfect example of how appearance can be misleading. Her green eyes are revealing a whole other side of hers, now she looks rather witchy as she eyes around with the look of hunter on the mission. I realise that she is also seeking how to jump the queue. Our eyes met for a fraction of second and she smiles to me with only her cute full lips as if acknowledging my presence; her eyes never stop constantly scanning the mob.

I turn back to see who is making noises behind me – again, a young girl, blonde, with cold skin tone, and cold in her demeanour. Her skin is white and matte like Chinese porcelain and artistic brown big eyes, which stand out in contrast to her otherwise Nordic appearance, quickly evaluating the situation. Funnily, with her thin bones and skinny slightly lordosis-like posture she looks more like one of those enormously expensive ball jointed dolls than like a human being of flesh and blood. She is miles away in her thoughts. Same gaze, same absent smile.

Another girl further behind her has an even more vicious glance that sends a chill through my skin. I unmistakably see total determination in her every movement; I suppose you may only come across such determination in kamikaze that are devoted to their duty and will not hesitate to end their own lives for a greater goal. Although this one is not slim, nor is she physically attractive, I am mesmerised by some inner force that she radiates. She has something about her that two other young stalkers don't, and I would have stared at her for some longer but I just don't dare. I sense the taste of aggressive competition here and simply don't want to provoke people unless I know what we are queuing for.

I keep looking around when a few people down the line start arguing and I am hoping I will get a glimpse of what is going on here. To my regret they speak a language that I don't understand; moreover I have never heard anything like that before. I have an impression that there are no vowels at all or, at least, not enough for human hearing to perceive the language as a harmonic natural language.

In such a situation I can only rely on the body language. The argument has something to do with the time – they bring their hands up and point to their wrists. Without doubt they both have obvious anger management problems and I also think how funny it is to watch the behaviour of irritated people – they weave their hands just like animals in their demonstrative fights so well documented in endless wild nature documentaries. People have added an extra twist to that – they speak loudly with all the muscles on their faces in tension; looks real funny! I note that they have strangely doomed eyes, like elder people whose wisdom makes them look fed up with life and somehow sad. I think is it the queue that made their existence unbearable – it must be.

I don't normally wear watches myself and don't feel them on my wrist now either. Nevertheless, I take my hand up in the same manner as them and drop a quick glance on my wrist – nothing. I decide to ask someone who, perhaps, will have a better idea of what is going on here.

I start looking around to ask the time from someone who looks at least a bit friendly. Unfortunately, I can only see all the same expressions as far as the queue go; people are scanning the crowd and when their eyes meet they smile briefly with the fake smile and turn away to the opposite direction. I note that a bit further ahead faces are becoming more doomed and hopeless; the waiting is definitely killing them.

After a while at the corner of my eye I note one elder man who sits by the pavement with no signs of wariness. His clothes are very old and faded and all look just various shades of sandy-grey; a bit more yellowish long cloak and rather darker peachy-grey scarf with some ornament that can't be grasped anymore. He doesn't appear to be in hurry anywhere as he sits motionless and absorbs this entire cavalcade. He definitely knows what is going on here and it stands out.

Realising that I will lose my place in the queue I try to call him but with no success – looks like he is either not paying attention or simply ignoring me. Argh, what should I do now? My curiosity is eating me alive! Thinking for a moment that he might have some private information I decide that it will be best to speak to him and find out, maybe there are shorter ways like guest lists or something. He well might be some kind of promoter; after all I know few promoters who have serious substances abuse issues so I wouldn't be surprised to see promoters dressed like that with an absent smile.

I make the step out of the line and hear some noise behind my back. They can kill each other for my place but I am not turning back. I feel very proud of myself that very moment as if I have made a very important choice. Even if it won't make me closer to the prize I still have finally decided for myself. I come closer to the stranger and to my amazement his face looks very young and is not imbedded with wrinkles – just some freckles from being constantly outdoors.

'Excuse me sir, could you please tell me what the time is?'

'It is not important what the time is; its important how much there is left.' Whatever he meant by that it didn't sound very promising. Looks like we will have a lengthy conversation here but hey, I have nothing to lose any more so why not to go along with the flow. Besides, everything about that stranger is rather intriguing.

In an attempt to satisfy my curiosity I ask another question

'Left to what, sorry?'

'Until it is your turn.' Well, I suppose it is quite logical conclusion, I wonder when can be my turn if I have already left the queue anyway. Are we talking about the same thing at all? Okay, I will play your game this time.

'Okay, how much time it is left please?'

'It depends; you may never even make it.' He replies neutrally. It looks to me that I have lost the track of conversation and am not entirely sure I understand what the discussion is about. He must be really enjoying playing mind games with me. Argh, why everything should be so hard?

'Depends on what? Sorry, am I missing the point here?'

'Depends on which queue are you waiting in, as always.' Oh now I see, we are clearly on the same page. Now I can recognise the promoters' jargon and feel myself more comfortable.

'So, I assume there are some fast-track queues here?'

'Yes, "fast-track queues", if you wish…'

'Oh that's what I thought, splendid; I was wondering if you could… recommend me perhaps or add me to the list if there is any… please?' I am feeling back on track and I have all the experience needed to convince the promoter. 'You see, I have left my queue right over there…' I point to the blonde girl who was queuing before me,'…so that I can chat to you and I would be very grateful if we can fix this small issue somehow perhaps?'

'Sure,' he replies, 'just tell me what are you after and I am sure we can figure something out. After all it is not nice to make a lady wait, is it?'

Oh, what a nice character he is! Of course it wouldn't be nice to make me wait in a queue, and by the length of this queue it might be a life time. He is indeed so helpful, bless him.

'Sure, right, what am I after? What's on… hmm, what's on offer, so to say?' I am trying to hide my ignorance under the cloak of politeness and it always works with promoters.

'You.' He smiles. He was surely waiting for this question and glad he can puzzle me.

I actually was prepared to name him several familiar clubs and restaurants so his response frankly confused me.

'Sorry, I thought for a moment you said it's me,' I say with some irritation.

'It is precisely correct.'

Okay, this guy exhibits obvious symptoms of dementia; probably he had too much last night and I don't even know how to help him or myself. What a situation! I have totally lost the trail and going back to the queue is also not an option; I will simply get disfigured. Okay, thinking logically: firstly, there are several queues with only me being on offer and secondly, I myself might not even make it there; what the hell is he talking about? Is this some kind of riddle?

'Do you want to say that all those people are here for me? Is that what you're saying?' I am not even trying to hide my annoyance.

'These were the ones who queued for same dream as you my dear but you don't have to worry about them, they are long gone now.'

I am totally confused. Where have they gone and why, and where are they now? And if they were queuing for the same dream could I get a piece of it, too? I look both sides hoping to see at least anyone sane – it is all empty; we are alone in the middle of nowhere, in the place with no coordinates. Something within me breaks down and I start begging him to bring some clarity.

'Please, please, would you *please* tell me where we are and what is this all about? Where are we and what should I do now? Where have all the rest – I am sure it was a lot of people here just a minute ago?'

'Well, there are always a lot of "people" if you wish. It's the labyrinth of Cronus.' He smiles enigmatically and combs his silver beard with fingers witnessing my face getting paler and paler.

I remember I once got lost in tiny maze at age of six, ever since then I hate mazes and I go absolutely hysterical when I see one. There is nothing I can do about it; I just start panicking and whinging, asking someone to rescue me. But before I can do or say anything he continues.

'You don't believe all those Hollywood movies, do you? No reason to worry, there are no monsters chasing you or willing to kill you. You are relatively safe here.'

'Relatively? Oh, that's much of a comfort, thank you.' I start looking around to get an idea of what are the monsters he was referring to and how to get out of here. 'This is not even a labyrinth! I can't see a single wall; you must be winding me up, aren't you?'

'This is a metaphor, you silly human being.' It sounds somehow very racist yet caring. He continues, 'I can only say this much, if you will find yourself running it's because you have chosen to. Time is the only trap you will find here. That is the only thing threatening you now and always.'

As he spoke his voice gained some momentum and in culmination he dropped down the cloak that covered him and I see a huge hourglass floating under his chin where his body should have rested; he is a one massive talking hourglass. The tiny particles of sand fall quickly to the bottom chamber forming a vortex on the surface in the upper section.

'Okay, time, got it.' Is there anything else I must know about him? I decide it is the right time to summarise our conversation and leave him 'So there is no queue and the labyrinth is just a myth; all who have been queuing for the same dream are "long gone", so, I suppose, I can just get what I came here for?'

'Not unless you will decide what you are after. Don't try to tell me you are here for the same reason as all the rest. You've been there and it didn't bring you anywhere nice, did it?'

He knows my weak spot and I start feeling absolutely vulnerable. Seems like I have no choice but to admit my mistakes and until then I will stay in this limbo forever. His white ivory-like teeth send a sparkle as he smiles.

'I will tell you what: you can only get in fast-track queue if you choose to be yourself; all the others are already taken... You will tell me how it went next time we meet.'

He snaps his fingers; I wake up.

IX

11.12

The morning began painfully, mainly because of the headache that had become my long-standing friend during the years of wild partying and consumption of various substances ranging from light wines to the killers shots. The headache is mixed with the overpowering sense of guilt for showing a wholly different face last night, and sprinkled with the icing of unbearable anxiety from meeting this daybreak (just the same as any other) absolutely alone. This is my usual morning cocktail I have to take each time as a fee for being a sociable and enigmatic seductress by night. What can I say? I am happy to pay the price because it saves me from the solitude for at least another evening.

For those few years I lived in the flat I got used to the void of silence that is sharing the space with me; the only sound that can interrupt my sleep is the agitating buzz of my phone. I can never be bothered to switch it off for a night as I get very disappointed to find out that I have missed something interesting and exciting. Despite having regular hangovers I prefer to spend my morning with a cup of something, somewhere nice, in the company of, preferably, attractive young men. In absence of the latter any living soul will do; anyone who can lead me away from my morning blues with their chatter.

This time it's only a text message from one friend of mine who happened to arrive in London today for couple of days. Just a usual text with his traditional auto-correct mistakes that are making me so annoyed. Anyhow, seems like I won't be alone this early afternoon. Obviously, this is not something to dream about but better than nothing.

The chap is travelling a lot and every couple of months he comes to the UK to look after my hair and share his usual moan about all and everything. Since I met him I have learned to switch off from actively listening; it turned out that not so many people actually care if you listen or not. All they care about is to pour their frustration out, release the stress and use a bit of your vitality. I know that and I don't mind, after all it's only fair as we both are getting what we want. Just need to adhere to the usual script and all will go smoothly.

11.25

I pop one painkiller; it will fix me by the time I am out of shower. I turn the cold water on to wake me up and try to recall what happened last night. Struggling to make up one continuous picture I give up. No memories, no problems I comfort myself.

11.57

I am having my lazy cup of double espresso in the garden in a bright sunlight with my mobile next to me – not bad company. A light breeze is playing friskily with trimmed bushes of jasmine, carrying around this truly delightful heavenly scent. I roll up my PJ shorts and sit right on the grass. What can be better than a sunny day – just a sunny day spent with your loved ones? Is it too much to wish for?

X

13.45

'I am leaving the country,' he goes. 'I'm leaving the place as I am sick of it…' He has put a guilty face on and is staring right into my eyes, right through me as if trying to guess what is happening in my mind; chilling. We are sitting in the same pub as several years ago, we always meet here but how much has changed since then. My mind gets flooded with memories of a naïve feeling of involvement that I was silly enough to experience back then. Three years ago we were sitting in that rear corner, having our usual G&T. Three times before that day we were meant to meet but every time he cancelled saying he had too much going on, his plane got delayed, his travelling arrangements have changed and all that. I wanted to see him then, desperately. Why? I was obviously silly and was falling into my submissive pattern of being a victim. Yet, something was different then, I have managed to let go. I remember I got so fed up with his excuses then that I was unable to even listen to the endless stories he would come up with just to squeeze some more emotions out of me. I couldn't empathise any longer – no compassion, no pity, no excitement; I couldn't be bothered to encourage him or feel in any way sorry for his miserable life he dreamed himself into. I didn't believe his life was miserable after all, it was all just a charade to make me feel something. If not admiration, then pity. If not excitement, then at least a bit of guilt for not being a good listener, anything would do.

Three years have passed and even today he is the same. This clown is surely expecting me to break into tears or at least to say I will be missing him ever so badly. Clown… I have never loved the circus and certainly wasn't much into clowns. I am biased against the jesters and can't understand how these characters keep earning money from kids while half of the toddlers are genuinely afraid of them. I think of how the clown outfit would fit him. No, my imagination paints him wearing this white harlequin kind of costume right now. Definitely harlequin, bring the comedy in! The costume fits his jelly belly and his always miserable face. Black circles around his eyes from the dim light are adding even more charisma and he is ready to serve the public and feed from crumbles of emotions lavishly spilled out by the masses.

I hear the crowd around me going, "Oh…" like in those shows with voiceovers, the support from masses he is craving for. I have only now realised that ever since we sat down he has been skilfully balancing on his imaginary one-wheeled bike. He has indeed mastered that talent, performing effortlessly. Interesting, does he leave his bike outside when he goes to the loo?

The menu on the table all of a sudden turns into a price list with each of his tricks having a price. I couldn't help but skim quickly through the price list, very handy thing I must say. The price list reads:

"I have left my girlfriend" – congratulations/pity – 10% of your energy level

"Yes, I finally got the divorce!" – congratulations – 10% of your energy level

"You were not listening" – apologies – 15% of your energy level

"I got new contract" – congratulations, pat on the shoulder – 15% of your energy level

"I am leaving the job" – genuine pity/congratulations, long pat on the shoulder – 20% of your energy level

"I am leaving the country"– sincere sorrow and regret of losing, pat on the shoulder – 20% of your energy level

"My ex-wife is going to court again to claim all I have" – 30% of your energy level

"I love my grandson so much and want to spend more time with him" – Oh bless him, empathetic expression – 20% of your energy level

God, how much did I want to finish reading the list! Realising that the rhetoric pause is getting too dramatic and I am expected to answer something I folded the menu and nicked it into my bag quickly; I will read it later.

Okay, so according to the price list I must pat him on his shoulder and show genuine interest in his business, and that is exactly what I would have done just four years ago. Instead of that I am thinking aloud: "I must call Harriet and see if she can do my hair then." Yep, that is almost the only reason I keep meeting with him now – I can't be bothered spending fortune on a stylist in London and besides, my hair is damn wicked – blonde, dry and curly so, unless there is an absolute emergency like that you don't really want to change your free stylist who can cut you perfectly with his eyes closed. And yes, this is the only thought that crossed my mind that very moment... After all, he is professional in this and I have even seen him in annual style books produced by one of the prominent hair care brands. Tough? It's life.

A bit chilled by my response he takes a break and sips his gin & tonic. The cube of ice in his glass made one last attempt to escape this whole extravaganza and somehow falls out on the table as soon as the glass touches hard surface. Picturesquely it hit the table and slipped on the floor; with a dull sound reporting the landing. Maybe it is the right time for me to do the same as, I am sure, my companion won't stop there, he never does, he needs his dope; sentiments, that's what he is feeding from. As if guessing my thoughts he takes the stage.

'I want to go somewhere warm and spend the rest of my life not chasing for my tail, you know. Enough is enough; I can't stand it anymore. Spend at least thirty hours a week on the plane.

You know it yourself, I wake up in the morning on Monday in Delhi and go to bed on Wednesday in Kuwait, then back to London on Friday for half a day meeting. And when do I get home? Once every three months or not even that, you know that.'

Oh yes, sure, I feel so sorry for you pal, you have such tough life travelling around the world giving some sales tips and some new haircuts, getting paid a six-figure salary and never worried about any expenses. Even this drink, I know for sure, will join the long list of your expenses claim just the same as those receipts left over on the bar counter.

'…I have told my boss today that I quit. After a month probably, and I said I am not going to India again. There is no way on earth I am going back to India, I hate that place. This is the worst place I have ever been to, I am telling you. I mean, how can you work with stylists and teach them something if they just don't bother to style their own hair? And, *oh god* that place stinks!'

At the beginning of the monologue his body language revealed some uncertainty but as he convinces himself more and more the voice becomes more confident and the body language shouts out that he will stand for every word. Yeah, right, you can convince that old man sitting in the corner with his pint maybe but not me. I have heard that several times now.

His voice fades away in my mind; I am not listening anymore. My mind is swamped with images of the training and seminar sessions he is doing in a hundred degree heat in a salon somewhere in Delhi balancing on his single-wheeler, wearing this ludicrous harlequin costume. All the stylists clearly realise that he is just another clown from distant Europe… no, from another planet, to say the least… But threatened by redundancy they must pretend that everything is just all right, they try ever so hard to not to stare at his bike. While some of them, especially eager ones, bring similar clown single-wheelers and hope they will get promoted. The bosses are, of course, giving the other ones their evil eye and so everybody is trying even harder to smile and pretend that they really enjoy the masquerade and that this arrogant chap will surely change their culture. Moreover, he has a smashing long-term impact on the sales in the region! In the evening however, when the comedy is over, they will all go out for a party and early next morning all repeats like de ja vu.

'… and you know I think of you every single day. Every time I wake up I think of you and every time I go to bed I think of you, I blame myself for missing my chance, I really do, you know…'

Whoa, how the hell did he get to that point? Did I miss something interesting? I am not surprised by the fact that he actually said that but rather by how quickly he got to the point. I must admit, he gets to that every time; this trick is somewhere at the bottom of his price list and it is the last resort to get my attention.

I am wondering that perhaps he must be getting older and doesn't bother to come up with new tricks or jokes to entertain me anymore; he is a really bad performer, and me… I must be really stupid to be paying for the same bad play over and over again with both my time and my verve. We repeat all the same ritual step by step, every damn time, no surprises and no motivation to change anything. Everything is just convenient enough for both of us to pick up the phone and type dull text and then just meet up again and escape from suffocating seclusion in exchange for some quasi satisfaction of our ill self-esteem. Damn, we both know what the Game is and whose move is next; when and what will be the next passage, and what will be the outcome… and nothing will ever change.

This idea is making me sick to my stomach and I am getting frankly disguised by all this foul play we are bound to perform every time. It struck me, so deeply in my mind and even beyond. Something that you can't explain or even describe, you just see it unfolding in front of your eyes and think how blind you were before, how could you ever buy into it? All our meaningless routinely repeated dialogues fall apart in small pieces like that ice cube few moments ago and it is not important anymore who is talking and what is being said. I can now clearly see the core, the pure fire-like impulse that is jumping back and forth between us, the raw energy. That is what matters, that is the only thing that ever mattered, and all the rest is just rhetoric.

I get flattered by the beauty of the mysterious flare for few moments. I think if that is exactly what happens every time I meet anyone or even more, every time I speak to someone? The invisible vibrant flame that extends for miles, reaches far beyond my five-sense reality; the puppeteer, the true reason for everything.

This very moment it feels like no relationship will ever be the same again. Now, when I have finally grasped the true essence of any interaction I know for sure what to look for. Forget the dumb glamour magazines and free pocket-size novels that were feeding me some nonsense for the whole of my life. Now I have the real tool, now I can finally trust myself in my choices and hopefully, trust someone else too. Someone special who has also seen the flare, someone who, perhaps, just the same as me got disillusioned with blown up reality called be-like-everyone-else-and-don't-try-to-figure-anything-out.

I let myself soak in a little bit more of this new insight and then just blow to the flame of this energy very gently until it dies away. That's it, no more games. For the first time in a long while my head is so clear, for the very first time I have realised what was this all about and once I got to the root I have no more intention to play this game.

'It's gone; I must also go now, sorry. I will call you later… not.' While I stand up the menu falls out of my bag on the floor and it appears to be simply two blank pages, no text or images whatsoever. I couldn't care less; I am not interested anymore.

That's it; no hugs, usual phrases or dull promises to catch up next time, I just leave. I just do what I have always wanted to. I don't need plan B and never needed one; I am finally being myself without fear of consequences. It doesn't matter either, there will be no next time and I know for sure I won't regret it, I won't be feeling this excruciating loneliness ever again and there is no point to be afraid of something that will never happen.

How absurd must have been all my efforts to work out never-ending back up plans without actually focusing on the only one thing that really matters – the plain vision of my happy self. Not the self who feels miserable opening eyes in the morning; distressed and terrified of the prospect of spending the whole of my life meeting one night stands in endless restaurants and clubs or even worse, trying to fix clearly broken people on expense of my own time. Not the self who is exhausted from relentless need to be entertained and dreadfully bored being on my own. Not the self who is sick and tired from being in perpetual fear of failure in my relationship; fear of not being able to love just right, or not to fit someone else's expectations that I have been told about in monthly fashion magazines.

But the self who is simply content and radiant of the raw unrestrained rebellious energy; the self who is not chasing for insignificant things being led to believe that the most important objects in life are impractical possessions of little worth. The self who knows the value of own private space and time and will never waste it for worthless affairs or straight-faced people…

The buzz of my phone wakes me up from my thoughts. The text reads: "Hey. Quick warning, my girlfriend (we're back together) found out we went for dinner last year when we were still together, she may message you about it on FB or something. Just tell her the truth that nothing happened, we just had dinner etc., sorry."

Whatever…

The smell of petrol mixed with strong oriental oud blending together in warm air, the usual Knightsbridge smell, embraces me and welcomes back like an old friend. I know, I know, I was so blind for so long.

PART TWO

I

05.40

This early morning he opens his eyes to yet another virtuous day. The sun is shining through wooden blinds right inside patrician bedroom leaving on the creamy Persian carpet parallel lines of light about forty-five degrees diagonal to the bed.

He closes his eyes and listens for the world in his usual fashion; he knows his territory by sound as no one else does. Outside there is the sizzle of tyres crawling down the paved mews and the sound of powerful Bentley engine, very quiet on a low speed but you just know it is one damn powerful toy. A bit further outside – the familiar quiet hum of the high street that is waking up from its night's sleep. The main sound is birds' chirruping and the whisper of tree leaves.

Inside the house, downstairs in the kitchen he can hear familiar sounds – clatter of dishes and mechanic noise of coffee machine; fridge door opened for few beats and closed again. It takes him not more than a couple of seconds to scan the situation; it pleases him to know that everything is just the way he knows it.

He wakes up and crosses the room towards the en suite bathroom. A refreshing cold shower is one of the usual morning rituals that unlike most of others haven't changed since he met Fiona; the bathroom is always free when Alistair wakes up.

Today is quite important day for his firm but it doesn't bother him much for everything will go smoothly as usually, it is just another day that is not worth worrying about.

There was a time when he had to prepare for every important meeting or conversation trying to think of various unexpected twists and how to respond, saving the face and reputation of the business or even better, how to put the opponent in a disadvantageous position. He used to rerun lengthy conversations over and over in his mind while in the shower and later in front of the mirror, and would even mumble something in the car while getting to work and then again, in the office. It was some odd twenty years ago. Now he doesn't need practicing or preparing, there is hardly anyone who could put him in a hard position with their questions.

Standing under the flow of water he takes his imaginary golf club, prepares and chips… hole.

06.07

He comes downstairs to the kitchen already dressed in a smart
suit and a snow-white shirt.

'Would you help me with cufflinks please?' He is addressing
a young, attractive lady who is blending fresh green juice.

She makes a half turn and smiles while still keeping one hand
on the blender; she is really happy to see him. The woman is very
good looking with thick, long dark hair, glowing skin and light
blue eyes that radiate charisma and happiness.

'Are you awake already? Sorry if I woke you up with this
blender; maybe we should check for some quieter options,' she
says, wiping her hands against a white kitchen towel. She presses
a round button on the coffee machine and helps with the
cufflinks. When the coffee is ready she takes a small cup and
passes to it her fiancé.

He takes the cup with one hand while with other takes Fiona's
palm closer and it kisses gently. A ring with trilogy diamonds
sparkles on her fourth finger in the bright morning sun that is
overlooking them both from the kitchen window.

Alistair is finally happy with life; this young lady brought sense
and fulfilment into his life and it is definitely a good change. He
is enjoying every moment with Fiona. It seems that she is also
happy; happy on her own, unconditionally and he is just lucky
enough to witness it every day. Ever since they met she never

showed that she needs him and this independence flatters Alistair, it is something you don't see often in young attractive ladies.

In addition she just understands him so well and knows what his needs and wants are. No, she actually has the same desires and goals, same taste and pragmatic mind; she is more like his reflection, his alter ego.

'Do you remember, sweetie, what we are up to tonight?' She kisses him and, not waiting for his response, adds, 'I am so excited to be honest.'

Pouring fresh juice into one large glass she takes a small sip.

'Mmh, this is so great, you must try it, I added a bit more kiwi today. Are you sure she will be up for this sort of stuff?'

Alistair smiles, how smoothly this girl moves in the kitchen. He always makes him smile.

'Yes, pretty sure; she mentioned once herself how she had an affair with one girlfriend and was positive about repeating it.'

'That's great, that's what I want today.' She winks playfully and laughs with ease.

Loosening his tie a bit he goes, 'I know I asked already, but is there no better ways to find a girl for a fun night?'

'Baby, don't worry, it will be all fine. I want you to find me a decent girl, not just any cheap whore and knowing your taste I can trust this into your hands.' She leans against the kitchen isle showing off her long toned pins.

The best thing about his fiancée is that she is a bit kinky and after he proposed they decided that it would be nice to find a beautiful girl for a night, one last time before they get married and it was the deal that Alistair will find someone to their taste. He loved this idea to start with and he was really pleased with the trust Fiona puts in him; trust is the best cornerstone for any relationship. However, at some point it started getting a bit awkward and he would rather pick a one night stand in their usual place.

'I know, I know, just thought we might find someone in the club as usual, would save me much time.' He puts the empty cup in the sink and hugs her gently so as not to spoil her perfectly ironed crispy shirt.

'C'mon, admit you like it, it's a kind of official affair and it will be rewarding, I promise I will take good care of you tonight. Besides, at this Killing Kittens they are all the same faces, I am frankly bored and I want it to be for real if you know what I mean. After all, you have already agreed to meet her so too late to turn back.' She sips from her glass and adds: 'I hope, as you said, what was her name, Chelsea, is good looking and has long legs. You know how I like it.' She smiles again. This smile always comes from somewhere deep within and always reflects what she actually means. She is playful today and obviously very excited; keen to have a good night and make him happy.

'Chelsea is quite interesting name by the way, I like it.' She adds. 'So, just to recap, you are going out for dinner together tonight.' She speaks while trying to sort something in her bag. 'Do you know where yet?' Not waiting for a response she pulls a rectangular dark grey card in matt finish with gilded embossed letters on it. 'Here, take that one. The place is truly good; I went there with Jess the other week. The food is delicious but don't be going there with empty stomach – you won't get full. Anyhow, I am sure you will like it; just don't be thinking of me too much.' As Fiona turns back to the worktop her pony tail jerks quickly.

'Okay.' He takes the card. 'I promise I will take you there next time if I like it.'

'Sweet; I know I probably don't have to tell you but try to keep her on subject; seduce her if you wish. Oh, what am I saying, you know better.' She is not even looking at him while loading the dishwasher with cups, glasses and the blender jar.

'Okay, all sorted, I will see you in the club in the evening then. Do you remember where we went last time, around Soho? It'll be the same place tonight.' She is putting her jacket on; one goodbye kiss and she is gone, leaving him in anticipation again.

A quick read through the morning newspapers and his mind is sharp; it's time to make a move.

II

06.53

Caught in traffic on his way to work, Alistair takes time to plan his day. It is a bit too early to call to the restaurant; PA Jenny can take care of it later, and one more thing he should remember is to ask Jenny to ask about the artwork he saw the other week. It was a very bright and somehow calmly dramatic abstract painted in striking red and calming creamy inserts. From the very entrance to the gallery this painting absorbed him as there were no other works in the gallery. He is positive Fiona would love it too. She will be able to appreciate the clean and sad splendour of that masterpiece.

12.15

The meeting went well, just as Alistair expected. All those meetings and negotiations became the usual thing for him since he found a way to keep business and emotions separately. Business is all about figures now, for sense of accomplishment he goes elsewhere.

Some time ago he used to find it very rewarding to debate on various subjects and felt real triumph when he succeeded in getting his point of view accepted by others. Not any more, at present his life is all about good quality time and people and, of course, Fiona. And if she wants a girl as her little guilty engagement present it is the least he can do.

Alistair truly enjoys his time with fiancée and all about her is just mindboggling. He likes the way she wakes up in the morning, always tries to rise first and sneaks out of bed quietly without waking him up; always fully prepared for the day by the time he comes downstairs. Fiona just doesn't happen to have this childish habit of idling in bed. By the time he comes down she will have read the major headlines and will elaborate on her opinion, making an extra effort to discredit biased media.

Of course he knows all that but it is just very amusing to watch how one young woman is trying to educate him and influence his opinion. She leaves absolutely nothing to chance, exhibiting almost non-human discipline and determination in everything she does. What entertains him most is Fiona's obsession with straight angles and lines, you can see it by the way she dresses and organises the room. Funny, she gets a particularly tough time organising the living room full of small bits and bobs, collectible souvenirs and trophies that almost drive her mad while she is trying to arrange them, guided by inner sense of perfection.

The picture from the gallery popped in his mind again, he wonders if this abstraction of uneven yet perfect lines and shapes will help her to appreciate that not everything must be aligned straight. He would love her to take time to soak in this picture and embrace the absolute raw perfection that can be found in chaos.

The melodic ring of the landline distracts him; it's Jenny on the phone.

'Alistair, I booked the restaurant for you for two. It's tonight at nine o'clock as you asked. Also, the Americans phoned while you were in the meeting, requesting a conference call. I didn't book anything as yet. I wasn't sure what your time scale is; please email Roger.'

'Thanks Jen, you are a star. One more thing, remember that gallery I told you about the other day, just off Great Titchfield Street? Yes, that's the one. Can you please call them and tell I will get the artwork, what it was called, *While You Were Awake*. I will settle everything tomorrow. Thank you.'

He sits for another moment in the quiet office trying to recap his actions. He could never imagine that the request of his wife would be so hard to fulfil. Of course, it is not hard physically, yet it is quite a challenge on so many levels psychologically. Here he is, a few months before the wedding in his late forties; completely satisfied with his personal life and truly in love with his future wife. Yet, there is something he needs to accomplish

– "an official affair", a true mission to seduce a young starlet and serve her warm on a silver dish for Fiona's amusement.

The seduction part is the easiest one: he has already taken a few steps and taken her shopping; it always works. The only real obstacle is that he feels really sorry for the young lady who is wasting her time on empty affairs or dead ends, as he calls them. Not intentionally, but he starts seeing through Chelsea and it is quite obvious she needs fixing. He sees the conflict boiling within her and there is no outlet to her frustration. In contrary to Fiona, Chelsea is still a baby with girly ideas and dreams; being a natural actress she skilfully hides it under the mask of feminine sensuality and, probably, is getting away with it most of the time. Alistair can read her character and he'd prefer he couldn't. He is seriously concerned that this evening will cause the remains of her fractured personality to shatter and the responsibility for that will lie on his shoulders; his and not Fiona's of course, she is blissfully ignorant of Alistair's concerns.

Never before he had taken personalities into consideration when searching for a quick sleepovers and one night stands and it was always easy, but something is different this time and it doesn't feel right.

'What needs to be done needs to be done.' Alistair convinces himself that this is the price that needs to be paid for the happiness of his woman. It's not that she won't be happy if it doesn't happen, but it will surely amuse her and, taking into account Chelsea's appearance, Fiona will be most pleased with his taste. Hopefully, the "dish" itself will enjoy the evening and he will add another victory to his long list. It will prove first of all to Alistair himself that there is nothing impossible for such an influential man.

'Enough, get on with your work pal,' he cheers himself up.

III

20.00

By the time Alistair gets home it is almost time to leave, just enough for a quick shower and to shoot off. Alistair dresses in silence; he prefers it that way because it helps him to concentrate.

He pulls out his evening suit wrapped in crispy laundry bag and a fresh shirt. Picking the first random tie he thinks it's not that bad, he can't be bothered choosing much. Besides, it was gift from Fiona so she will be there with him in a way. Alistair likes the idea of wearing his woman's gift while "hunting for a prize." He is a hunter after all.

On the way out he adds the evening fragrance to finish off the look.

21.15

Of course Chelsea made him wait; he expected that. She seems to be that kind of lady who thinks that getting there late is the new fashion as opposed to bad manners; never mind. She looks gorgeous tonight, her matte skin looks fresh; Fiona will like it. Push up bra under a tiny cocktail dress that hardly covers as much as it should; she knows how to wrap herself up to tempt any man.

Chelsea apologises acting a bit like a little girl and says her watch is five minutes behind. Alistair is not a big fan of Marilyn Monroe kind of characters, but what can you do; here she is and she is damn sexy.

'You look great tonight. I am actually lucky I am sitting right now otherwise you would have a chance to literally see how glad I am to see you.' Alistair doesn't lie; he is very excited envisaging a night full of lust and pleasure they are moving into. He can't wait to see Fiona and her reaction when she meets Chelsea. As odd as it may sound, he really wants Chelsea to have a good evening and enjoy it together with them.

The restaurant suggested by Fiona has impressed Alistair – the quality of service and the food itself are second to none. The interior is also comforting, with dim lights and more private seating where you can enjoy each other without being distracted. What must have attracted his fiancée most is the interior design; no Rococo or Victorian style nonsense, only sleek modern fittings with interesting lighting solutions. Feels like you are somewhere in New York and not in heart of Mayfair.

Fiona definitely has a good taste and as promised he will book a table for them sometime next week. This very moment Alistair really misses her and their long intellectual conversations. Something that he values most about Fiona because everything else will fade with age but not the way she expresses herself.

Regrettably, in Fiona's absence, he'd better focus on Chelsea and make sure their conversation is all about guilty pleasures.

At some point, Chelsea excuses herself and Alistair starts worrying if the girl is all right, maybe it's not the best day today after all. In fairness Alistair is not even sure if Chelsea will be back and as such he uses the moment to text Fiona and let her know that plans might be changing.

Her response reads: "Don't worry too much, darling, see you in KK alone or with C. I am having couple of glasses with G. Can't wait to see you. Xx"

That gives him a bit of comfort. It is nice to know that you are loved and accepted regardless of the outcome. It is also uplifting that there were no notes of jealousy or naiveté in her response as Alistair finds it easier to deal with mentally grown up people who always mean what they say and are not playing silly.

21.45

When Chelsea comes back she looks calm and content again; demonstrating full awareness and readiness to go beyond the boundaries this evening. She would pick very intimate details of her life and play around with words to captivate his imagination. For a moment he even believed that he was wrong about her. After all she might be actually happy and wholesome in her character.

'Good for all of us,' he thought.

They drank some wine and then they drank some more. They spoke for a while and although she didn't seem to be up for a talk to start with he managed to find another facet to her personality. Chelsea is really knowledgeable when it comes to not-so-much-mainstream mythology; her explicit understanding of the sequence of events in the ancient world is impressive, as well as her ability to draw parallels and see things as uncut. This knowledge cross-pollinates with her clearheaded awareness of the present and the fruits of such brainwork are constructive and at times cynical opinions and suggestions. She hides it well though trying to fit herself into the frame of a valueless world, a frame she created for herself.

It' a shame he is able to understand all that because today he would rather be unsympathetic and just deliver what he promised. As for Alistair, he would prefer to spend another couple of hours in the restaurant and then get her a cab home. In hope to hear a refusal and to grant them both a last chance he wonders if she feels like going out at all. Not knowing what she is agreeing to, Chelsea is determined to carry on with the evening.

23.15

On the way to the club she slipped down the seating a little, pulling her already short skirt even higher. She doesn't even seem to be preoccupied by the way she looks and he can't resist the urge to kiss her on the shoulder. There is something in her that lures Alistair, something he can't explain. Her authenticity perhaps or, it well might be simply the fact that he understands what she is made of, her fragile world of dreams and disappointments.

23.32

By the time they got to the Killing Kittens, Alistair has serious doubts that he has the right to simply do what he has to without feeling guilt and pity for this young female. By that time he truly is attracted by her psyche and the idea of just using Chelsea is not sitting well with him. The only thing he wants is to see elegant Fiona again, and all those doubts will disappear in a moment, he knows for sure. He will most likely even laugh at himself tomorrow recalling this evening and his hesitation.

They take seats downstairs and enjoy some drinks while he scans the crowd for sight of Fiona. Although everybody is wearing masks, he would spot her even entirely wrapped. The waiting becomes unbearable; the dialogue is growing in his mind. Alistair really considers telling Chelsea off and saving her from a real mistake. He can read her makeup and although Chelsea can easily submit to Fiona's pleasure tonight, she will most definitely regret it tomorrow; and there will be no one to help her out.

Here she is; her familiar slender body appears in a crowd. Fiona wears black underwear and a long evening blazer that barely covers her buttocks; high heels are adding grace to perfect physique. She nods acknowledging their presence and appreciating his choice. For whatever reason she decided that it would be best to join them upstairs and just socialises in a crowd for some time, avoiding any direct contact.

All Alistair wants now is to pass Chelsea over to Fiona and let her deal with it from then on. In fairness, the chances are Chelsea will be up for this affair and, given the circumstances, somewhere deep inside he wishes for Chelsea to turn them both down; that would be the best way out for her. He would never have thought that at some point in life he would wish someone to turn his fiancée down. And what is more bizarre, that it would happen even before the actual wedding.

Alistair tracks Fiona with only his eyes and follows her as soon as she goes upstairs. There she is, in the company of some more friends. He comes closer and although their appearance might have looked rather odd no one will ever say a word; the unwritten rule of the place.

Pretending that they hardly know each other they start the usual polite chatting with glass of something. Fiona favours champagne and Chelsea goes for a stronger mix. Alistair is used to the setting just the same as everybody else apart from Chelsea. It is so obvious that he starts worrying it might be too much for the gullible girl but before he gets to ask her how she feels the young lady leaves to go to the bathroom.

Miniature slim blonde in short dress walked away to the ladies' with unsteady steps, trying to not to look around. As Alistair understands it, now is the most important moment for her today, or maybe even in whole life. Now she will make the decision and either will come out as lady-vamp or as beaten puppy; he is eager to see which one will win. He consumes the moment of anticipation as Fiona comes closer and kisses him for the first time since morning.

She is totally oblivious to what is going on in her target's mind; she laughs and gives him credit for picking a very attractive young lady with a sense of dignity, particularly describing how amused she is by the way Chelsea feels shy in this surrounding.

'This is even better than I expected she whispers, thank you sweetheart; I knew I can trust you with everything.' Fiona embraces him and inhales his perfume. 'I was missing you and was almost a bit jealous. Almost.' His fiancée is in complete emotional balance as always and he can feel it very well.

'As promised I will take good care of you tonight,' she whispers and kisses with a deep tongue.

As they kiss, Chelsea comes out from the toilet and approaches closer. Alistair is not sure now whether it is good she saw them or not. In any case, it has already happened and sadly, he missed the moment she walked out of the ladies' room. Was it as a convinced seductive diva or a beaten and miserable puppy – he will find out very shortly.

All he can do now is be the guest of this evening and enjoy every bit of it regardless of the outcome. Alistair relaxes and lets himself go with the flow with two pretty ladies surrounding him. He embraces the fragile body draped in the tiny silk dress while Fiona puts her hands on Chelsea's shoulders as she usually does; probably the only one calming gesture of domination. It calls for trust at the same time as it demands for surrender. Alistair has seen this gesture working over and over again; there is something he learned from Fiona after all.

In an attempt to pull Alistair away, Chelsea almost falls down. He knows it means she made up her mind and won't be staying a minute longer in here. But instead of letting her just go he uses one last chance to infuriate her, so that she wouldn't leave beaten and miserable but rather with all her emotions spilling out. Anger is destructive, but misery is even more destructive with its long term impact. All the anger and doubts that we don't deal with are accumulating within us, seamlessly impacting on our future responses and judgments; best is to have it all out and move on.

'Are you okay? Your childish behaviour is embarrassing to say the least.'

That was just enough to break her; you can see how her face changes and her pupils went wide black while she is trying to think of the response. Now she will reply and fight for herself like a lioness.

He is not listening for anything she says; instead Alistair thinks that no matter how painful and insulting her accusations, she will never even scratch the surface. If only she knew the whole truth, that she was just a request of Fiona's. In truth, Chelsea is just another one of Fiona's toys for the night; quite beautiful and expensive but still a toy.

The lady who he is about to marry stands by his side and squeezes his hand in an attempt to prevent something ugly happening, not realising that the ugliest thing has already happened and it is how she herself looks in light of all this situation.

Not waiting for Chelsea to leave the room, Fiona breaks into laughter.

'Did you hear that, what a jester! Well, at least she's not like that other one last time.' The blazer slipped down her shoulders. Seeing some unease in Alistair's eyes she adds: 'Oh, don't worry, I am not upset at all.' She loosens her bra and kneels in front of him. 'I told you, I will take good care of you; your night is just beginning, honey.'

Alistair is miles away as he tries to sort out conflicting thoughts. The rose-coloured glasses through which he was looking at Fiona fell down and shattered in small shards. All he sees now is how egoistic his wife to be actually is; ready to use people for her own amusement.

Fiona, in truth, is absolutely unable to empathise. Thinking about it she never mentioned to him that she needs him or never showed her more human side, never cried or been upset. Her every movement is planned well ahead and there is no place for feelings in her heart. Everything she ever does is for her own benefit. Everything. Him too?

No, it must be just alcohol; Fiona must be a great person no, she is *definitely a great person*, always with perfect sense of balance. He swallows doubts that leave metallic taste in his mouth and closes his eyes.

'Long term impact… we shall see.'

IV

Next day, Alistair goes to the gallery first thing in the morning. He absorbed *While You Were Awake* for what felt like an eternity and it convinced him yet again that this was definitely the right choice; everything about this canvas captivates him to the point where he perceives his life to be a part of this abstraction; complex and twisted in its own way. It is distorted yet absolutely perfect with each element having its own place.

'Yes, I will definitely take it,' he addresses the administrator of the gallery.

'Sure sir, very good choice. Shall I send it to your home address, sir?'

'Yes please.' After a short pause he asks the administrator to hold. He takes out his mobile and navigates through the messages. 'There it is. Send it for the attention of Ms Chelsea Scott please. Here is the address.' He shows his lit mobile screen to the administrator.

'Any note to go with it, sir?'

Alistair scribbles something on a blank sheet of paper.

'Just this one.'

The note reads:

You've done well, thank you.

Alistair leaves the gallery, out into the warm summer rain, full of thoughts. He decided he wouldn't be going to work today as he needs some time on his own.